DESTINY

ADVENTURES AWAIT...

ABHINAV MALLAM

ISBN 979-888546212-9

For all my family and friends, who encouraged me to write this story, complete it, and publish it.

Well, no. Not REALLY. HAHAHAHA! IN YOUR FACE! Just kidding, I love you all guys. Sike!

Contents

Foreword

Fantasy is a genre of speculative fiction involving magical elements, typically set in a fictional universe and sometimes inspired by mythology and folklore. Its roots are in oral traditions, which then became fantasy literature and drama. From the twentieth century it has expanded further into various media, including film, television, graphic novels, manga, animated movies and video games.

Fantasy is distinguished from the genres of science fiction and horror by the respective absence of scientific or macabre themes, though these genres overlap. In popular culture, the fantasy genre predominantly features settings of a medieval nature. In its broadest sense, however, fantasy consists of works by many writers, artists, filmmakers, and musicians from ancient myths and legends to many recent and popular works.

I am too inspired, from the stupid boring stories of all time that make me want to go die in a fricking hole named tartarus, but when I put my hands on my first ever fantasy books, I WAS ADDICTED.

Preface

There is nothing really there to read here...Just skip onto the next page, I hope you like the story!!

Acknowledgements

I don't have any acknowledgements...HAHAHA! It's not funny, I can tell it. Don't worry :)

Prologue

The day never stopped when I started world war 3. HEY! It wasn't my fault, but the day seemed to be there. The night never occured, And I was scared. Did I do something, Like- Destroyed the moon? Oh Monkeys, I am dead. Probably most of them whould think I was the kid who caused all this. But guess what? It isn't me. I was just a simple 19 year old boy who went to St. L'manfer's college. I didn't graduate yet, Don't bully me.

The craziest, most brutal mission you ever go is on a Destiny. A real life destiny.

It is some, dangerous mission where I just go training and go get introduced to a bunch of small troops.

No rescue, no diffuse, no plant. ONLY KILL.

Think of a FPP game. You see like it's all shooting, killing, and stuff like that.

Think of something more BRUTAL. Like weapons that can kill you in a shot, and you're dead like a dead field mouse.

Dangerous mission, gone by the NSTL, (No second to live) is the worst possible company ever to be created on earth. Kills you in no time, I say.

So how I got into this mission is kind of a long story, and I do NOT want to tell you.

But, I guess you deserve to hear it.

Lets go-

WAIT WAIT WAIT-

Have I mentioned my name anywhere?

No, right?

My name is- Robert Lewis, But you can call me Rob.

I was just so scared.

I had nothing to do.

No family,

My dad a monster and my mom a who-knows-what.

It shouldn't have ended like this,

OR maybe, It shouldn't have started like this. Let me start from the beginning.

Like- The beginning of the beginning.

CHAPTER I

Are you the PIZZA WOMAN?

Ever saw a brutal war?

That's what I am seeing right now.

In a T.V, don't worry.

Just getting to the best part is so EPIC, but it gets RUINED, when someone rings your bell at the exact perfect moment the DUDE CHOCOLATE kills the enemy.

"Oh look at that, this is SO annoying." I muttered to myself.

After I opened the door, I wish I fainted and was admitted to the hospital with a report that says

--Died of Mental Fear--

1997 to 2021.

Dying SUCKS.

Oh look at that. When I opened the door, standing in front of me was a girl, wearing a blue jacket with red gloves on. She wore a white shirt inside the jacket that says-

EXAMS GO BRRRRR

Goes bad alright.

She had red eyes and brown hair.

She looked like a warrior that came to kill me right in my house, and me who missed the BEST part in Legends of War.

Her expression looked REALLY serious.

"Uh, Hello? Here to deliver the pizza I asked?" I asked, a little nervous because she had a KNIFE, whose handle poked out from her jacket pocket.

"No. I came to warn you." She said,

"Warn me from what? WORLD WAR 3?? HAHA! Nice joke, but no thank you. Bye."

I said, laughing a bit madly- I guess.

And I was just about to close the door right on her face, but she said- "I can buy you The Legends of War 4 EXCLUSIVE edition. If you come with me." She said, smirking (See, that's how you lure me into something.)

I stopped, holding the door.

"Don't LIE." I said.

"I'm not. I'll really give you, if you come out with me, and I tell you something SECRET."

She said, raising her eyebrow.

"I don't wanna hear any secrets, like, you're gonna tell me, I'm born with a father or mother as a GOD? Or maybe you're gonna tell me that I'm like some stupid chosen one on some WEIRD adventure or blah-blah-blah." I said, TOTALLY COOL.

"Nah, you're right about the ADVENTURE THING, but-

Wanna know something more DANGEROUS than mystical adventures?" She asked, TOTALLY COOL.

This HAD to be it. I like dangerous things. But what could be more important, something that is more dangerous than a SUPER-DANGEROUS MYSTICAL ADVENTURE itself?

"Hmm. FINE. Meet me tomorrow. 8:30 AM. Hokie's Coffee." I said, raising my eyebrow, because that girl seemed kinda suspicious.

"Alright." She said, her expression kind of relieved.

"Bye, Robert Lewis." She said, waving her arm slightly and walking away to the Elevator.

HOLEY HECK. I thought.

HOW-

DID-

SHE-

KNOW-

MY-

NAME?

Including my surname.

Okay that's enough. I thought.

Maybe she was a friend of my mom,

Or a friend of my friend's friend.

Or someone who I DON'T know.

Don't take it too seriously, Rob. You're just out of your coconut mind.

I said to myself.

Well. Coffee shop it is.

You know, The one thing I hate is COFFEE. And I don't even KNOW why I asked that weird girl to come there. But one thing for sure. I won't order coffee. Even if someone offers me a billion dollars for it.

Anyway, feeling puzzled, I went back to my room, watched some stupid soap opera, and went to sleep.

And also, one more thing I need to say about myself.

I get DREAMS.

Oh go on. You're gonna OBVIOUSLY think that I'm gonna get BAD dreams. Read stories like that?

But NO.

They won't tell me the truth. But they will tell me the FUTURE, of myself, or someone I knew and was close to me.

Most of them are about that they get hurt.

But NO, they never get hurt. In fact, they're perfectly fine.

So, assume that they are stupid useless dreams that go into my mind every SINGLE night. Just to torture me, I guess. Or maybe even make me irritate myself and scream like a monkey on the bed, tear all the pillows, open the fridge and eat all the food- (Kids, Don't steal food from the fridge, or your parents will slap you to death).

Yes. I steal food from my fridge.

If I forgot to tell you this, I'm living ALONE. That's probably why I hadn't mentioned that someone else is in my house.

My mum and dad went away to some other place, just to visit my relatives.

But they didn't return.

It had been weeks, and they still hadn't returned. I tried calling them, but the stupid device says that their mobile phones are switched off, and when I asked my relatives, if they were there, they would simply say-

"No Robert, they never arrived here. Maybe call the cops?" They asked. I get the SAME answer.

I was getting annoyed.

So I closed my eyes, my ears, pulled the covers, and slept peacefully.

JUST KIDDING.

OF COURSE not peacefully.

So erhem. Lemme tell you what kind of a horrible dream I got TODAY.

So uhmm

It PROBABLY went like this.

I was in a very VERY dark room. Which I don't like. I hate closed spaces. I hate the dark-

Lemme just continue.

Yes, as I was saying, I was in a dark room. There were some pictures of old people, who lived THOUSANDS OF THOUSANDS of years ago.

But some were like, from 1500?

I recognized Shakespeare, Henry Hudson, William Pen, More. They just seemed to stare at me.

And then there was a table, with a lamp on it. There was a chandelier on the ceiling. And there was a clock, on t-t-the other side of --gulp-- me.

I don't like grandfather clocks. They kind of CREEP me out. There was a little noise, which woke me up from my DREAM, and I saw my greatest fear right AWAY.

CHAPTER II

That was not funny, Jake.

Nah, Not a monster, or some thief coming into the house, getting a gun, pointing it at my head, demanding for money, then rickrolling you. It was JAKE.

"Dude, Dude, DUDE, DUDE! WHAT THE HECK! Why are you here, in the middle of the NIGHT, and just a question, how did you open the door--exactly? I locked it." I said, totally shocked, with my arms covering my face like I'm protecting myself from super radiated sunlight.

"Just, to WARN you." He said, ominous.

You need to know this JAKEY-JAKE. This guy's totally clever, and he's well, lives on the top floor. There are 25 floors, and I live on floor 3. NO WONDER he came down 22 floors just to WARN me?

He wears a cap, wears glasses, has FRECKLES on his nose and wears a green shirt with a dinosaur head that ALSO says--

WE ARE NOT EXTINCT!

they're not.

"Warn me from WHAT?"

"From something--That's a secret. I need to tell you later. Meet me somewhere." He said, nervously.

"WHAT'S UP WITH YOU GUYS? This evening, around 7:30 PM a girl knocked on my door. She also warned me and said that it's a SUPER sacred secret, and I told her I would meet her in the coffee shop." I said, looking sternly. Also terrified. WHY I was terrified? Because JAKEY-JAKE will come and knock on my door in the middle of the night while being totally OMINOUS and trying to warn me from--Scary? OR from telling me to stop eating chocolates from my fridge? NO ONE can stop me. Unless you think so.

"WHO? Was that? a ------------------Girl?" He asked, his expression even more terrified.

"Yeah, But I should go, even though I don't want to. Because she offered me Legends of War 4 EXCLUSIVE edition. For FREE." I said, drooling a little bit, then coming back into my senses and wiping off that saliva from my mouth. (Yeah, sorry. It's disgusting. But I always have an interest in games.)

"NO, NO ROB! She's a traitor. She-she-she. Just tell me how she looks." He asked, his eyes widening.

"Jacket, white shirt, red eyes, brown hair, bad attitude, blue jeans, having a knife in her pocket, making a CREEPY face, and all stuff I can't explain. JUST tell me what's wrong with you? You never went this terrified except for when you threw a rock in Mr.Mason's house but it hit the doggie?" I asked, looking at that scary, terrified face of Jack.

"We need to EVACUATE this city RIGHT now." He said.

"HOLD UP, HOLD UP. Why? FIRST OF ALL, what's the secret? Tell me right here." I asked.

"Can't. Sorry." He said.

"No, close the door, lock it. Eh, like that. Yeah, spin it. Good, okay. Now tell me what's so scary about that girl and what's the secret you were about to tell me." I asked.

"Alright... Here goes nothing!" He yelled a little bit.

"SHHHHHHHHHHHHH."

"Fine, here. Look, I know NEWS, about your parents okay? I know where they went, why they were missing for about 2 and a half weeks, and why they weren't lifting at all." He said, his lip quivering like he just saw a real dinosaur.

"Woah, hold up right at that moment. WHAT do you know about my parents???" I asked, in disbelief.

"They-they uh, They went to the coast of Cubic Island." He said, now his head dropping.

"Wha- wait. There's nothing like Cubic island." I said, now thinking it is a JOKE.

"No, no no. I knew you would say this. It is hidden. Somewhere. It is almost impossible to find." He said.

"Alright. Jokes on me. What's so SPECIAL on that island, and why were my parents going there?" I asked.

"No. They weren't GOING there. In fact, they were going to your relatives house. But, They uh, got lost in a storm. The hexagonic storm."

"Dude, stop lying and go to your house. Or I'm gonna call your parents." I said.

"No, you have to believe me. She- That girl, she's evil. She's taking you to the CUBIC ISLAND. There are fights on that island. They-- They take you back in time or they take you to the future. They make you kill someone else they've captured. They will ask other guys to kill YOU. They, Oh my gods. Legends tell that that was an ancient battlefield. The island is hidden by a big advanced technologic shield, that makes the island invisible,

From the rest of the world." He said, now his eyes in wonder.

"So. You want me to believe this?" I said, my eyebrow up.

"Yes-NO- JUST, believe it or not, you don't dare go to that coffee shop and meet the girl. She might just kill you. And the thing you mentioned? That knife? That's just to kill YOU. ESPECIALLY YOU." He said, then without listening to my response, he slammed the door and went away. What the heck happened to him NOW? But I guess I should or shouldn't go to the coffee shop (I shouldn't

Believe me.)

Yeah. He's well, I don't know. Maybe he lost a few marbles and maybe he's telling me his dream, by mistake? Well.

Shouldn't think about it much. Right?

(I can see the coffee shop right from my window.)

And there I fell on the bed. Took my warrior figure, examined it, and slept.

----------------RINGGGGGGGG!--------------

"WHAT THE-" I almost screamed and jumped out of the building.

Oh. Don't worry. Just the alarm. You don't want to fall and die out of the building. Do you? I thought.

Uh. "UH UH UH UH UH UH UH UH UH," I mumbled.

Yeah. Right.

Gotta go take a bath.

So I ripped out my covers, threw the action figure somewhere only god knows, and ran inside the bathroom.

Probably 5-10 minutes passed?

Who CARES? I don't CARE.

I quickly took a look at the calendar.

YES! SATURDAY! A HOLIDAY FROM SCHOOL!

I quickly jumped on the couch, took the remote, and switched on the T.V.

"GO! GO! GO ON HUNTER MAN! KILL JUSTICE NOOB!" I screamed, even though my neighbours wouldn't mind the thrashing and screaming coming from my house.

"Yeah. Oh wait. I hadn't made myself some breakfast." I said, frozen.

"BAH! Just some cereal. How much time does it TAKE? Heat the milk, throw the delicious cereal, sit on the couch, and watch The Legends of War series.

25-50 minutes later.

"PHEW! Took a lot of time. Or I would've killed myself." I said, grabbing the cereal and keeping it on the table.

WAIT. How many episodes have passed since I went for cereal?

"NO, NO! 2 episodes ALREADY?" I yelled, almost for everyone in the world to hear.

"Oh wait. I can rewind." I slapped my forehead and rewinded back to episodes.

-ZZZZZZZZZZZZZZZZZZZZZZZZZZZZZZ-

"Huh?" I said.

The T.V started snowing. Like, when you know, it goes all black and white.

Suddenly, a man's face appeared on my T.V screen.

"Hello, Robert. I am General Hrockut. I am here to escort you to Cubic Island. My men are coming soon. Please wait for them." He said, and disappeared in a twik.

"WHA-" I stood, my jaw hitting the floor.

So, is Cubic Island REAL?

No wonder, that JAKE said it was true.

BANG BANG BANG BANG!

Suddenly a sound came from my door. "WHO'S THERE?" I shouted.

"We are the general's SOLDIERS. And we will take you to CUBIC island, where you will meet your worst FEARS."

CHAPTER III

I escape the Legends of Cubic.

You can't take me nowhere. I'm the stealthiest ninja in this world. -BANG BANG BANG- "COME OUT MR.LEWIS! I'M GONNA TAKE YOU WHERE YOU'RE PARENTS ARE!" Someone shouted from outside the door. He's gonna think I'm gonna come out of the house because I want to see my parents? DUH, no. "No way." I said.

"ARGHH!!!" A warrior shouted.

BOOOOOOOOM! Suddenly the door exploded right near me, but thank the gods it didn't kill me.

And then, I saw a man. His eyes full of yellow and buzzing electricity. His axe was marked with ancient teqweraq words, And a armor made of pure light.

"You. Have no way to escape, Mr.Rob. We are the champions of Cubic Island. Or you may call it, `Terror of Death'." He said, seriously.

"Yeah, Fine. Whatever that stupid island is, I DON'T CARE. At all. No answer for me, eh?" I said.

"Then I'm gonna have to zap you." He said, with some snickering from the behind group.

NO NO NO NO NO NO! I thought.

"Well, If you will, I mean, if you would, look behind? There is a master of almigh- I mean, Master of Gods, RIGHT behind YOU." I said, a little nervous.

"WHAT! TURN BEHIND!" came out a sudden gasp in the group. Before you could blink your eyes, they turned around and were looking for him like Gone Mad by Kerzogatic Gerald.

Time to run.

I quickly closed the door and stood on the edge of the window. Oh no, I'm gonna fall out there and die, even though it's 2 flo- WAIT, it's 2 floors only! I CAN handle that pain.

So without hesitation, I jumped out of the building.

In my mind, I thought- It's okay. You lived a good life... I-I never regret this.

And then, I felt every bone in my body crack like crackers in a big boy supermarket.

"OW." I squeaked.

I looked at myself. It seemed FINE. I wondered why I heard cracks when I jumped on the ground.

I looked beside me and saw a KID, munching happily on Rocky's YUMMY chocolaty, hot, deliciously made CRACKERS!

"DUDE." I said- barely in a whisper.

"THERE HE IS!" Someone shouted from behind me.

My stomach froze into ice. I turned behind just in time to miss a sharp rock hit my face. "AHHHH! I MISSED HIM!" The guy shouted.

Then one guy with some kind of fire powers broke the wall of my house and with a fireball hit he made a crack on the ground. "HOLEY--" I shouted, barely missing a Hot FLAME hitting my face and Burning my face. TO ASHES. "OH my GOODNESS!" I shouted. And then without another thought I started running from the screaming gods behind me.

"STOP HIM! HE'S RUNNING TOWARD 12th STREET, BATLEY SQUARE, ALBANY, NEW YORK. QUICKLY SEND A DAMN COP HERE AND TELL THE DUDE TO CATCH THE BOY!" Screamed the Thunder Dude behind me. I never really expected to see a REAL-LIFE god using a modern-day human made mobile phone.

Can you outrun some gods who are trying to take you to some real-or-mythical island?

The answer is NO. It will never be YES.

Then I saw some cops. They were frantically searching for someone or something. I thought they were gonna help us and save me from the gods, but I was mistaken when I saw their guns pointing at ME.

"STOP. WHAT ARE YOU DOING? YOU'RE SUPPOSED TO PROTECT PEOPLE. DUDE, ARE YOU EVEN A COP?" I shouted to the two cops standing in front of me with their guns raised, lasers pointed at my head.

Behind me, all the gods surrounded me. Some people caught notice of what was happening, and started RUNNING. "SOMEBODY HELP!" I shouted as loud as I could to someone who was nearby and ready to help me.

No one. "You can't run away from us, kid. YOU NEED TO COME TO THE ISLAND." The thunder god said menacingly.

"WHY? You're no god. What's so good in it? WHY are you taking me?" I said, now covering myself with my hands, afraid where the lighting dude might hit me.

TOO LATE.

He hit me in the heart, and I FAINTED. First of all, I thought I'm gonna die. How can someone hit the HEART, and not DIE? Trick question. I did not die. So I'm IMMORTAL? No, lol.

After I woke up, I wished I fell back to sleep. I was in a cargo plane, for sure. There were boxes containing SECRET RECIPES of something DANGEROUS. They smelled like a year old SOCK.

All around me, there were the gods, or some other idiots.

The Thunder dude came in front of me-- And suddenly, out of nowhere, some ROPES came and caught my wrists and my legs. I was breathing heavily, something burned in my throat, and my stomach was EMPTY.

The Thunder dude removed his FACE, only I realized it's his MASK, and saw a NORMAL HUMAN's face in it.

"WHA-" I was about to say, but then he shushed me.

"SHUSH, SHUSH, I'm not a GOD, you fool. Just dressing up. And it's not a thunderbolt either. It's an Electricity Spear. We are not gods at all! WE ARE THE LEGENDS OF CUBIC ISLAND." He said JUST those words and injected me with something RED, and I fainted.

When I was back, I was in a BED. I was in a huge room, with red walls, paintings of great warriors. There was a huge chandelier on the ceiling and it was TOTALLY RUBIED. The room was very cold, and there were many beds, with other people too. Wow. So happy to have company. All had a thousand- I mean 5 glasses of lemonade, just beside them. The room looked good. But I was still a bit scared.

"HUH? WHERE AM I...?" I yelled a bit, then realized that I was very very weak.

"I uh, will tell you." Said a sudden voice.

"WHAT?" I turned around to see who it WAS, and was surprised.

"Jake?" I said, my mouth open and my eyes HUGE.

"WHAT! WHAT ARE YOU DOING HERE! HOLEY MOLY!" I screamed.

"Yeah. Nice to meet you too Rob!" He said, with a weak smile.

"Oh my gods! Where did you come from? What are you doing here! HOW did you come here???" I asked, a thousand questions buzzing in my mind, but I deleted it from my storage--Err, I mean, removed it from my mind.

"Well, First thing. BANANA."

"Banana?"

"Yes, BANANA. That's how I found you. WITH THE HELP OF A BANANA!"

"Wow. Great.." I said, a little disappointed.

"See, after I ate an apple, I went to throw it in a garbage bin, but saw a sign.

'BANANA AT YOUR APARTMENT ENTRANCE!' It said, and I was petrified.

Well, I came back to my senses and went to the apartment entrance. Sure enough, there was a banana near the photo studio, and I went to pick it up. Just when I TOUCHED it, a dog came out of NOWHERE and snatched it. I turned just in time to see you, running from some crazy people with weapons, and I followed you.

Annnnnnnnnnd so they SAW me, captured me, gave me some drink and I fell asleep, surprised to see me here and more surprised to see EVERYONE ELSE here, ETC."

"WOW."

"Cool, right?"

"No."

"Seriously."

"Yes."

"Okay."

"NOW, tell me where I am?" I said.

"I think we're still in the cargo plane, just in another section-Pretics 56.

Saw the sign."

CHAPTER IV

The Hexagonic storm

"Oh, well. That's a disappointment. Also, these gods aren't gods. So you can't think of them as gods because they AREN'T gods at all. So stop believing them that they are god-"

"I did not even trust these noobs."

"Okay. But it's rude to interrupt when a person is speaking."

"No. I'm rude."

"Bad boy."

"LOL"

"Okay."

"BANANA."

"I don't like bananas because they are bananas."

"Can we stop these useless conversations?? I'm seeing a storm." Jake said, lazily.

"Oh. There isn't a window?" I enquired.

"I mean, I heard a sound. Which sounds like a storm. If I'm not mistaken, THAT, is the HEXAGONIC STORM."

"You sure?" I asked, a bit VERY terrified.

"Yeah, COMPLETELY SURE."

"Okay."

'ATTENTION PLEASE. I MEANT ATTENTION. WE ARE ENTERING THE HEXAGONIC STORM. SO HOLD ON TO SOMETHING UNLESS YOU WANT TO DIE. Ehe. ALRIGHT. NOW GO CATCH SOMETHING! MUHAHAHAHAHAHAHAHAH'

Said the speaker, that was very much near to my bed, which made my ears bleed.

Everyone was frantically searching for something to catch on, and found SOMETHING. I looked around myself and suddenly a girl around my age came running and hit my hand, said sorry and went to catch a pole. "People have no eyes, I guess." I said, very quiet.

"What?"

"Nothing. Just sayin-"

"Nah, it's fine. Cmon! Found somethin' to hold on to." interrupted Jack. I guessed he had no intention of arguing in the middle of a life and death choice.

'Alright, you foolish people-' began the speaker, but someone yelled something in Spanish, and I took that as 'SHUT UP!'.

'Alright, alright. Ygnai, what is this? Don't talk like that. I KNOW, you just want to win a fight don't you?' asked the speaker, as the room became more and more quiet. REALLY quiet, I say.

He said something in Spanish, and I understood that. 'Yes, but I have NO idea where you are taking us? You said that you'll take us to an island, and now you're saying there's a storm overboard and now we're all gonna die? Came here for no penertable reason? Oh come on! DOES ANYONE WANT TO GO WITH THIS MYSTERIOUS SPEAKER?' said the dude, fiercely.

'Alright, My name is Jeffe, and I AM, warning YOU. We're going to the TERROR OF DEATH, where you learn to fight, grow up, strengthen, and fight the Doomsday coming soon. AFTER, About a month, the biggest villains that ever lived on this universe invade earth, and we-- experience Doomsday. If you don't fight, no living species will ever live on this planet. EVER.

Also, the storm is known as the HEXAGONIC STORM, and it covers the island, which makes it invisible from the people who spectate new adventures in the world.' It said, now in a more kinder tone.

'FINE! BUT I CAN'T DIE THERE! I HAVE A FAMILY!' He said, in Spanish of course.

'Oh, it's fine. They are well... easily...' His voice changed into an infrequent tone.

'Found...anywhere...' He said, but got interrupted. "ALRIGHT, shut up and say properly, idiot." Said someone in the group.

'We have health kits that once you touch, you will heal up in a second. Also, you can spawn them by clicking your wristwatch, which will be given when you reach sector 597 or the main lobby.

Okay, so uhh, we're entering the HEXAGONIC STORM, which is known as a shield or a cover on the island to make it invisible from other organisms from spying on us. Or even from breaking and entering...Don't try that.' He said, and laughed.

"Okay. But... I don't feel so good about the storm. If it IS invisible, how can I see it? Or even someone must have passed through it...Right?" I asked, feeling a little stupid because I was the only one who asked the speaker, also calmly.

'NICE ONE MR. LERIK! Yes-'

"It's Lewis."

'Whatever, just listen. Anyone who had not been chosen by our guards, and if they pass through it, they will pass through it as mist. See, that's a great shield, right!!' It said.

"Okay."

'Oh, I guess we've...Entered the New Era. The Hexagonic Storm.' It said, now laughing maniacally against the speaker, by which his voice was breaking.

"JUS- Tell me what's your name? MYSTERIOUS SPEAKER?" asked someone who had grey hair, swords on his back (YIKES!) and a face like a handsome monster. Well, he probably watches too much anime, because his eyes were glowy white. First, I thought he wasn't a living being, then realized it's just an illusion.

'My name is-- WAIT, didn't I already tell you exactly? DIDN'T YOU PAY ATTENTION?!?' Screamed the speaker.

"No."

'WHY! WHAT WERE YOU DOING!'

"Eating."

'From where did you get something to eat?'

"I already had something in my pocket--A chocolate." He said, now smiling, like triumph.

'YOU IDIOTS!' Shouted the speaker to some guards, or should I say fake gods.

'WHY YOU DIDN'T CHECK HIM PROPERLY!' He shouted so loudly it echoed through the room and almost made me run screaming.

But you CAN'T.

Cuz you fall out of the plane with no parachute and DIE?

No.

Never of course. What are you talking about?

"Uhmm sir... We uh, FORGOT, to bring Security Sectors. Left them at BASE." Said the guy with the Electrical Spear, which was now charging.

'UGH! Nevermind, JUST, everyone, we passed the HEXAGONIC STORM, and we, now entered, The Terror Of Death.' Said the speaker, his voice boiling angry.

"Oh alright, Lets see how it looks, Rob." Said Jake, beside me, leaning out of the window and his face totally darkened out by the dark clouds.

"Okay. Pumpkin sucks." I said and leaned out.

Have you seen a beautiful sight yet?

Is cool.

That was no terror of death.

IT WAS THE BEST!

It had a volcano, which spit out golden lava, and there were so many big forests one dude cannot resist to look and explore, probably even die there in peace. (Just kidding. Don't do that, last time warning ok?)

It had many sections and war battlefields, many bases with some kind of weird creatures and humans.

First of all, It was really good.

Second of all, I didn't want to be here.

Third of all, It was kind of scary to see humans riding fire breathing dragons and destroying an ice giant.

Cool.

It was just going good, until the pilot screamed.

"INCOMING!!!"

CHAPTER V

Are you serious? Like Really?

Are you serious?

What just happened?? AHHH, Alright, I shut up. Nice one. He was joking. UGH! Wanna kill him?

But of course. Yes. something moved near us so rapidly, all I saw was stormy grey eyes.

"Storm Dragon incoming, turn tilt plane 45 degrees. Safe mode switched 'ON'.

I got the right thing of COURSE.

"HAHAHAHAHAHAHAHAHAHAHA" The pilot laughed so stupidly, then turned the plane and landed on a clear sunny landing road in a huge wild airport.

Everyone got down and came outside.

The rich smell of wildlife came inside my nose.

"Wow. Okay. Can't believe I came to a thought so mythical island." I said to Jack.

But he was busy studying everything.

"OOOOOOOOOOOH WOW! LOOK AT THAT! FERNS! THEY WERE EXTINCT!"

He screamed, while I stopped him from calling a fully-grown ARK TYRANNOSAURUS-REX.

Jeez, that thing looked scary.

Someone came out of a well polished futuristic cabinet and greeted us, which I didn't like much.

He was wearing a white coat with a white hat covering his face, and his black tie was shining brightly in the sun. He wore black shoes.

I hate that guy.

He looked kind of a BAD BOY.

"Well WELCOME!" He shouted, the sand flying behind him and turning into a Sand Giant.

"RAAAAAAAAAAAWWWWWWWWWR!" It roared, making half the people jump and run screaming with fear.

"Aww, how cu-"

"RUNUNUNUNUNUN!"

"No. Don't. He's just a stupid sand giant. He doesn't even know how to close his fist." He said, his face so dark and calm.

"Okay."

"Gregor! NOW! Into your cabinet! SO STUPID!" He screamed at the sand giant, which now had a sad face and was going to a volcanic room.

"Mango Cheese." Someone said,

"Mango...Cheese...? Nice." I said, VERY VERY quietly you can't even HEAR.

"I know, right?" said Jake.

Too much for my silent voice.

"Okay."

"Okay, now you can CHECK OUT THE ISLAND! Just-- Try not to die in the wild, pretty ferocious griffins roaming

Around there. Look out for their talons, or...Front legs." He said, brightly smiling, In which his white teeth gleamed in the light.

"Okay." Said someone, the same dude with those ninja swords, or... I forgot his name...

WHATEVER.

Just chill.

It's easy to get killed by a bunch of weird creatures and all, but HEHEHEHEHE, what if you can kill THEM?

What am I talking about...

Let's just get to the POINT.

Yes, We got kind of a free time, allowing us to explore everything. First thing, I liked everyone. They seemed kind and waved and shouted 'HEY! HOW YA DOING?!' at me whenever I passed them. There were farms, huge buildings, people-- Wait, REAL LIFE people.

That's cool now.

I've been longing to see humans on the island, and I really wanted to ask how they got here.

See, it's easy.

There was a boy and a girl. OF COURSE.

I went over to them, and the first thing I asked was-

"How did you come here?"

"Oh umm, We got here by the Legend Transporter." A dude with mechanical spears said.

"WHAT- I mean, there's nothing such as a Legend Transporter," I asked, my eyes fixed in a question mark way.

"We'll tell later. Just meet us at lunch today-" He started, but I stopped him.

"It's evening."

"Right. Meet us at dinner. We'll tell ya everything tor!" He said.

"What's tor?" I asked.

"Nothing, just a habit of him." Said a girl, with white-blonde hair and a serious expression. She had a blade that was cracked with magma liquid.

Ok, OK, FINE. I admit it. That blade looked pretty cool.

Also, I didn't like the way the girl looked at me. GREAT CHOCOLATES! She looked like she wanted to kill me.

But, Nuh-uh-uh!

No one should kill me. OR I kill them.

Wait, never mind. I'm kind of weak. (Don't bully me.)

"Name's Gamora." She said, rubbing the blade with her hand. Must be pretty hot to touch.

"Okay. My name's Rob." I said, my eyes half open because the sunlight came directly into my eyes.

"Alright, Meet us at dinner. We got more of us."

Great. Now I'm having a load of friends. That's a good thing, probably they can help me escape this monstrous island...

So I walked and walked till I was probably dead and fell down on the ground, I saw the sun set.

Bad idea.

As soon as the sun disappeared from sight, a scary, bewildered howl filled up the night. This howl made me jump and run for my LIFE.

"HOLEY BUCKAROOS! WHAT WAS THAT!" I asked JACK, who was now riding a WarBat.

"Uhh, I don't really KNOW, probably a big bad wolf." He said, his smile widening to a nervous state.

Weird sounds came from the jungle, and a fire lit up in the middle of the jungle.

Literally all people went in there, and I guess I went in there TOO.

SIGHS

My LUCK. It was just dinner. I didn't feel too bad at that time, so I kept quiet.

The dinner place was so COOL! It was just like a campfire place, like the campfire in the middle and some logs around it, not just some but hundreds of them. Everyone sat on the log, and I did the same.

The SECOND I sat on my spot, The guys I met in the evening came and sat beside me. Instead of two, FIVE people came.

They all were wearing a dress called- LEGENDS OF TERROR.

Nice.

So let me introduce them.

First, a boy named Zack.

He had brown hair, totally combed, black shoes, a bit taller than me, wearing a white shirt with a heading that says LEGENDS OF TERROR.

OF COURSE.

Second, The girl I saw.

Third, the dude I saw.

Fourth, a big half-Troll that's double my size.

He's HUGE.

He didn't wear the same shirt that everyone wore, but wore a huge shirt called-

TIRED OF DYING? DON'T DIE.

OK,

And the last one, probably the leader, was the coolest.

He wore a king's CROWN and a necklace which must've been a million dollars. He also wore the same LEGENDS OF TERROR shirt, and he had awesome sunglasses.

SO he asked, "Alright, new boy. Wass' yeh name?"

"Robert."

"Alright ROB..." He said, but stopped. He just STOPPED, and he stared at me in icy silence.

The only thing you could hear was the crackling of fire.

Finally, what seemed like a bazillion hours, he stood up, opened his arms, and yelled,

"WELCOME TO THE PARTY ROBERT!!!"

Everyone broke out in a cheer and danced like crazy, and I, who didn't understand anything, sat on the log, confused by what happened.

Maybe this island isn't that scary.

I woke up, and was going to them, but suddenly, yet another-

BOOM!

This boom shook the entire jungle, and sent a repulse of energy, and I fell down, my vision going blurry and probably the last thing I saw was everyone hitting a LEGENDARY REPTILE.

CHAPTER VI

The Lord of the Jungle arrives.

When I woke up, I wish I went back to sleep. (I know I said this many times.)

A HUGE roar erupted from a distance. This ROAR sent some of the trees flying and a huge wind blew against us. All the campers were totally scared. There was chaos everywhere. There was blood, dead pumpkins, and a beautiful apple, but someone just stamped it.

The trees moved, The birds flew away from us, The ground SHAKED.

OK, sounds like the big cheese is coming now!" I whispered, agitated.

"Stop, TALKING! OR WHISPERING!" whispered back Gamora, SHARPLY.

"WHY! IT'S A LIFE OR DEATH SITUATION! I DIDN'T EVEN LAST ONE DAY HERE!" I said angrily.

"YEAH, I KNOW." She said, NOW TOTALLY angry.

We stared at the volcano for a few seconds.

Must've been an HOUR.

YES, it has been an hour.

The people looked a bit relieved. All the people went back to their partying as if NOTHING had happened. "Uhh, WHAT? A beautiful apple just got BROKEN, and you say it's USELESS?" I said,

to the KING.

"Oh yeah, Donna worry! We just woke the Jungle Lord, but uh, It's okay. He's back to sleep. But the thing is, He'll wake up 2 or 3 days later.

We've got time. But we gotta train all the new people who arrived, but. One problem, Yo." He said, now his face a little tired.

"We-we can't train all of them at once. So, the people who didn't get to train, will probably, -" He said, and without telling me any more, went to the deep jungle, and left me alone standing there.

I just knew what would happen to them. I looked at the new people, dancing and laughing like crazy, a few hours ago they were like- Wanted to go home, not fight this DOOMSDAY, So uhh, We- LOST.

I guess, I really felt sad about what happened to their lives; THEIR OWN LIVES.

Well, we'll try to figure it out.

Okay, So now, I went to the deep jungle to find the king. The jungle was so dark that I couldn't see much.

The trees were thick and branches came from the ground, making me trip.

Flies zoomed around everywhere, and the moon shone BRIGHTLY.

All of a sudden, my green eyes lit up. "WHAT- HOLD THE HECK, MAH EYES! NO! OH GOSH, NOW WHAT?" I screamed, my voice echoed through the silent jungle.

ROARS *CAWS* *SCREECH*

Yes, My eyes went into Night Vision.

"Woah, I never knew this. Probably because I never went out at night, or maybe at night there were many lights.

Sure, I am no longer human, I guess.

I AM A LEGE-

ROAAAAAAAAAAAAAAAAAAAAR!

"WHAAAAAAAAAA!" I screamed, as a mighty ROAR erupted.

I looked behind me, and saw a huge SABER-TOOTHED tiger, approaching me, growling and making nasty saliva.

"LOOK, I am no-NO- Threat. I uh, went to find the lord-- KING, I mean, who went to eat ice-- I mean, went into this jungle. Er, PARDON ME, but uh, Did you see that guy?" I said silently, my hand covering myself, and my legs whimpering. The leaves crunched below the tiger as it circled me, bent low.

"OH, have ya seen any---uhh late MOVIES?" I asked, hoping it would say YES, and leave me alone and go home.

But, UNEXPECTEDLY, it pounced on me and threw me somewhere-- 12 feet away.

WHOOSH

I hit the trunk of the tree and probably fainted.

I woke up, 2 seconds later, REALIZING that the saber tooth tiger was running towards me.

Now my anger rose up boiling. It was super RED and my hand gripped something.

I looked at my hand and was shocked to see a SWORD, no wait, a GOLDEN LUMINOUS SWORD, in my hand.

It glowed like pure gold and smelled of the wild. Some ancient writings were embedded there, and I knew what it meant.

'The Sword of the Wild'

HOLEY-

Did I just summon the sword of the wild?

For a second, I forgot all about the saber-tooth. It pounced at me, and I slashed the thing in two. I didn't even slash it hard, It was just like cutting cream cheese. So smooth.

It felt good, actually.

The saber-tooth lay dead in front of me, and I just stood blankly. I thought of calling for help, but I guess somebody knew to come here.

"What just happened?" someone said, and I turned to see it was the king.

"KING?"

"HOLEY--

ROBERT? What are you doing here! Why's a sword in your hand? And oh my- why's THERE A SABER DED IN FRONT OF YEH!" He screamed, and probably, I FAINTED, AGAIN.

Must've been hours after I woke up.

I was in a pink room. I mean, The room's walls were pink.

There was a huge + in front of me, and

And a load of campers circled me.

"Is it TRUE? He summoned the ancient Sword of the Wild?" came whispers from the group.

"Yeh good, mate?" King asked me.

"Yeah, I uh- There was a sword in my hand..." I said, now waking up from the bed.

"I'm fine, thanks. You all can go now." I said to all the staring PEOPLE, and then they went away, crossed the room, and their voices faded.

"So, what happened to me?" I asked the king.

"You just fainted, and the sword disappeared."

"What?"

"Yes."

"LOL. That thing... Did I summon a sword? The Sword of the Wild?" I asked, nervous.

"Yeah. YOU GOTS TO KNOW. That hasn't been summoned for a millennium or longer."

"Woah, cool. What does it do? Anythin' special?"

"NOT ONE, HUNDREDS! I still can't believe that you summoned it last week."

"LAST WEEK?"

"Yeah, why askin'?"

"I'd been here for a WHOLE week??!"

"Yeah."

"Sheesh."

"Alright. Here yeh go. It has the power to summon the Jungle Lord, he's now friends with ya. And then, you can turn into ANYTHING with the sword in your hand. Then you can have all the ELEMENTS of nature, cool right? AND EVEN MORE."

"AWESOME." I said, after he completed to tell the powers of the sword.

"I know, right!"

"Another one, you have lightning, fire, water, I LOVE water, and finally, Earth." King said, now moving to the more comfortable position near the couch.

"WHAAA! But, can the sword TALK?" I asked, feeling stupid.

"No."

"WHY?"

"Just- NO. It's not Magnus Chase. IT'S YOU." He reminded me.

"Right. I guess I have the power to summon the sword whenever I want?" I asked, a little disappointed if he said no.

"Yeah. TRY!" He said.

"MMMMMM... How do I summon it?" I asked.

"Seriously, being the son of a Lord of the Wild, yeh don't know how to summon the sword?" He asked, his hands limped.

"Nah."

"Jus' - concentrate, remove your nightmares, your dreams. Concentrate on your anger. Who you wanted to kill the most." He said.

So I did. I concentrated on the boy who stole my ice cream, who hit me. I hate that idiot. So I did as directed. I felt a huge golden whoosh over me, and-

Well, when I opened my eyes, THERE IT IS!

HowlDanger, the Sword of the Wild.

"YAHOO!"

CHAPTER VII

Doomsday Training.

Yes, James (One of KING's friends) told me that DoomsDay training starts tomorrow, and it had been delayed because of - you know. I ALMOST GOT KILLED.

So- it starts TODAY. Weird, right?

Well, just listen.

Doomsday training is really hard, and if you could do it perfectly, you need years of hard work.

HA! You'll think I can do it?

No. I also need training.

So it all went in a weird way.

6:42 AM in the morning

"Right. It is time I get off from the MEDICAL thingy and go take a look at my room." I said to myself after I exited the Care for Campers Official Station.

I met KING on the way to my cabin's room.

"HEYO! Wassup, you good?" he asked, slurping his slurpee.

"Fine...Yeah. By the way, where is my room? Just wanted to take a look at it before the training thingy starts." I asked him.

"Ah, I knew you would ask. Go into that department over there, and tell the receptionist witch - 'I need a DRAGON pet.'

Then she will give you one, pretty sure a magma type (Too common :C) and -" He said, but I cut him off.

"What do you mean I have to ask for a DRAGON pet? I MEAN, I need to have a dragon in my room too?" I asked, my mouth in a very trembling way.

"Nah, that's only for extra protection to campers. That dragon will also act as your key." He said.

"HOW?" I asked.

"Mmmm, let's say, it has a key in its HANDBAG, and don't you ever dare to check inside. Or you're toast.

Yes, and it has a KEY in it's handbag, there are a lot more in that thing, and it uses that key to open and close your door." He finished, and I wanted to protest so badly that it was the weirdest way you could think of a security thing.

So I didn't want the KING to kill me, so I had to shut my mouth and say - "NAH, It's awesome."

So I told BYE to KING and went to take a look at my new room.

After I reached the street, I saw the building. MAN, It was so TALL and huge that you might need 500 years to build this thing.

It was like- well, I don't know, 5000 floors? It was probably the tallest building in this island, or the whole WORLD, itself.

So the building was pure gold, and the thing was so luxurious.

I went inside an automated door and went up the path to meet the receptionist.

OF COURSE she was a witch.

OK, look. I don't really like this place much (Deep inside my mind) . IT all has things that are imaginary and not real. These things creep me out ANYTIME I feel like someones-

"Hello... HOW MAY I HELP YOU?" Came a cold voice from somewhere. I turned around and was relieved to know it was just the receptionist.

She was creepy, too.

She wore a purple dress with some dark purple designs.

She wore a pointed hat with a green emerald stuck in the middle of the hat.

Her nose was as long as a foot and her skin was very pale and full of pimples.

I didn't like her much.

So I asked for the dragon, and I got EXACTLY what KING told me I would get.

A magma-fire-breathing-type dragon.

The dragon screeched and sat on my shoulder.

SHEESH, I trembled a bit and headed for my room.

When I reached the floor, a dude named John came and hit my elbow, said "LOSER!" And went to the elevator.

See, that's what happens when you try to be nice and be HAPPY.

So I kept it casual and when I reached the door, the dragon checked into his hand bag and took out the key, and then opened the door. JUST when I was about to see how the room is inside, a sudden ALARM RANG.

"DOOMSDAY TRAINING IS STARTING! GET YOUR BUTTS HERE!" Said the voice, and well, I sighed.

This thing is not magical anymore. And I should've said this before, this thing really is the LAND OF TERROR.

So I closed the door, and headed out of the bunker, and reached a place full of futuristic stuff.

All the campers gathered there, like someone is giving you free PS5's.

I came near James, who put a hand on my neck and said, "WASSUP MAH MAN!"

"Yeah, well, hello to you too." I said, as that was the only thing my throat could give.

A dude with red tentacles on his back arrived on the front of the group and screeched in a toad like voice.

"WELCOME to doomsday training.

Here, you will train." He said.

"YEAH, we know." Said someone.

"Cool, now, you will be standing in a container. Please stand, no wait, it will come to you. Just stay STILL." He said, and chuckled, and giggled, and cried.

"Heh."

After a few seconds of ABSOLUTE silence, A few containers dropped from the sky from who-knows-where and each container trapped each camper.

"So now, good luck!" The dude said, and vanished.

"Wait..WHAT? He did not even SAY what these deadly containers DO!" Said Nakuro, and he slammed against the glass.

Suddenly, the whole container started vibrating. I felt as if my whole body was turning into particles, and whoosh, I felt cold air around me and I VANISHED.

6-7 hours later (Maybe 0.17 seconds)

I dropped from the sky, and I landed facefist on the ground. I woke up and saw it was SAND. "Hmm? Where AM I?" I yelled, but was a little disappointed to see no one answering back to me.

"YAAAAAAA! ATTACK!" Said a voice, and before you could turn, a huge spear double the size of me flew past me. A few inches and I would be dead.

I looked behind to see a HUGE army of GIANTS rushing at me, fully covered in Iron armor.

"YEHEEOOO!" Screamed one, but I was pretty sure I didn't get that.

I thought about something sad and suddenly, HowlDanger appeared inside my hand.

I used the sword to change into a SUPERGIANT myself, and in seconds, I felt as If I touched the clouds. I opened my eyes and HOLA! I was triple the size of a giant and was touching the clouds!

Now it is EASY.

RIGHT?

I put back HowlDanger behind me and rushed at the giants.

I stamped, I kicked, I punched, I wobbled, I threw, I YELLED, I sobbed for fun, I destroyed and finally-

I was face to face with the king of the giants.

EASY.

I kicked him in the stomach, but he dodged and punched ME in the legs. A burning sensation grew in me and I fell to my knees, FULL in pain.

But somehow AGAIN I woke up and hit him in the head, and he fell down. *dies*.

"HA! NOOB! CRY!" I screamed at the dead giant.

"GET REKT!"

CHAPTER VIII

SparkPlug Island

Well, I didn't even have enough time to celebrate though. I wish I had.

After I killed the stupid, ugly, monstrously, idiotic giant, I vanished again and this time, I landed on a island. I took out HowlDanger and turned back into human form.

Where was I NOW?

See, I hoped I would go back to Terror of Death and enjoy that super hot warm HOT TUB, but well, SAD me.

I was on some pretty happy sand. I looked behind me and saw that there was a jungle. I looked in front of me and saw water stretching for miles.

No escape.

Now what do I do here?

I thought I had nothing else to do so I just went into that forest to find some food.

GOSH, I was SO hungry.

And, THAT's where I found where I was. I found a sign board that said- 'SPARK PLUG ISLAND'

Huh, what a weird name.

I wonder why the tentacles dude sent me here.

Do I have to fight anything?

Do I need to scream for help?

Do I need to fall in the sand and roll in there and try to get all 'MUDDY' and scare my friends?

Do I need to give up hope and DIE?

Well, none of the options seemed great, so I just went back to hitting the board.

Finally I managed to make the board just CRACK, but unfortunately, It fixed itself.

"WOAH, is-"

THWANG

And well, BYE! I died.

Hope you liked the story!

Heh, just messing with ya.

Some arrow came and poked me in the chest, and you know what I did (FAINTS).

Yeah, I did faint.

So while I was DYING (I just hoped I died. A peaceful death in some sparkplug thingy.)

I was in a repair shop.

HMM? Some people were forging, and some people were repairing.

But the thing is, they weren't humans. You could think they were elves.

It was all fire, the hotness, the flames, the sweat, the fear.

I knew it all.

Someone then just burst opened from the door behind me, and it was a familiar face. All elves turned toward him and their faces turned into fear.

"I hope you all are creating them?" The man asked. His voice was RASPY, and it was totally evil.

He walked in a weird way, Just think- He LIMPED.

The face came closer to me, and finally I could see who he was.

I couldn't believe my eyes. I wanted to cry out. I- didn't know it was my dad.

"KILL THEM ALL!"

Well, see. I wasn't expecting that my dad was some evil monster trying to kill the entire population of Terror of Death. And as well as SparkPlug Island's.

SHEESH.

Well, what 'bout my MOM? Was she also a terrorist?

For some strange reason, I couldn't feel sad or angry.

I didn't know what to do.

So I just thought of something happy.

Well, ROB!!!

Welcome back buddy! HAPPY BIRTHDAY! Today you get to kill some monsters, while I kill the entire population of the earth! You just sit here and watch some YouTube videos. Nah, nah. Don't worry about me. I just have a doom gun that destroys you all.

Ah, wait. You want some chips?

JUST ASK MAN!

Well, I'll go get it.

D'you want something else?

A human head?

A human eye?

Bad idea.

After some million years, I woke up.

My eyes soon opened little by little.

AAH!

Gosh, I had the sun shine directly into my EYES.

I love my eyes. Beautiful eyes.

I slowly woke up from what I was resting on.

My chest hurt a lot. The pain flared all the way to my head, which gave me a lot of headaches.

"Who the HE-" I was about to speak, but someone put a cloth on my mouth so I couldn't speak.

OW.

I finally shutted up and turned to see some WOMEN, and they were whispering about me.

They wore some traditional dress and had angry looks.

What did I do now?

One of them came to me, took out a huge lava spear, poked it a inch from my throat and whispered, "WHO ARE YOU?"

"I'm Robert, and I'm innocent. Just blame it all on that tentacle dude, he teleported me here. LOOK, I'm no threat, and I would like to go back to Terror of Death." I said, nervous.

"WHAT is the terror of Death?" She asked.

"MMMM, well, it's some kind of a huge island with human eating monsters, giants, scorpions, dragon sized mosquitoes, and more." I said, now even more nervous.

"Very well. Get out." She said, her eyes again angry.

"That's rude, But yes, I'll go." I said, not looking at the woman in case she might poke me.

Then I took my sword, which was unharmed and safely kept on some table.

I went outside and the warm light of the sun hit me, I knew this was one great island.

I looked in front of me and saw loads of tribal people, with sticks and swords, preparing for something.

They knew about the DoomsDay or what?

Some people even had human technology.

Cool.

I went to one of the nearest tribal dudes and that was an old man.

"Hello, sir!" I said, and he turned toward me.

"¡Hola! ¿eres nuevo aquí?"

Well, he spoke spanish.

So I explained everything to him.

"¡Hola señor! Soy Robert, y acabo de llegar aquí, quiero decir, teletransportado aquí. Acabo de ver a esta gente. Entonces, estoy pensando, ¿estás entrenando para la gran guerra o el DoomsDay?"

Yeah, I knew spanish, learned in my 2nd grade.

"¡Sí! ¿Cómo lo sabes? Estamos en grave peligro, así que entrenamos todos los días. Ayer vinieron algunos muchachos a comer algo, creo que cuatro de ellos.

¡Ellos también eran como tú! Se teletransportan aquí por error. Tenemos un rey aquí, tienes que ir a conocerlo." He replied, and I was pretty shocked. Some other dudes came here, like me?

So I knew I had to find them, And I was 100% sure that they went to the king. So I asked him which way to the king's castle, and he said to go to the west.

It was a pretty long journey there, But I managed to cross the village's borders and on my way to the castle, I saw a weird creature with wings flying behind me.

It landed in front of me with a slight wing movement and TALKED.

"Hello! I'm a microraptor." It said, and I didn't even know what to say after hearing a microraptor TALK.

"I, uh- am Robert, and uh, I need to go to the king's castle or something. Can you move?" I asked, not to be rude or anything.

"Well, nice to meet you! I'm Oscar, and I can take you to the king's castle in no time!" It said,

Hmm. Very suspicious. What if it is a traitor, and threw me from the sky? It takes at least five seconds for me to turn into a bird with HowlDanger.

But I really needed to get there fast, So I accepted the offer.

I climbed on it, which took me MINUTES, and with a countdown of three, we took off.

BAD CHOICE. It took me VERY FAST!

So I realized it was too late for a drop off, and thought it would be best if I sleep. And really, I slept. Peaceful.

CHAPTER IX

Oh CMON! HOW MANY WARS?

Yeah, right. The air was peaceful, The grass was cool, But I missed my home. I wanted to just go home. Why did I even get this sword? I better throw-

Screech

AH! A ball of fire raced past me.

Maybe, nevermind. I need the sword. Maybe when I get home I can dump the sword somewhere.

All this fantasy is messing with my brain.

In a few weeks time, I'm gonna forget math.

I'm not LYING of course.

So after I woke up, I saw a huge gold castle. They were embroidered with some uhh, Well, I don't know what you call them.

I finally got dropped in front of the castle.

For some weird reason, there weren't any guards, or armies in front of the castle.

So I thought I was a VIP and entered the castle.

YOU might think it would be crazy if I became godzilla and destroyed this palace.

But I don't know. If the guards were hiding somewhere and they found me, they might come and shriek, HA! Caught you, you arrogant child of the wild god! Such a wimp!

I didn't wanna get bullied.

I kept HowlDanger at the back of me so that it indicates I'm not to harm anyone.

I saw that the entire castle was gold, even the furniture, lights, carpets, sheesh. Something in my head said, Duh, of course everything is gold. Are you senseless?

No.

So without knowing I searched the entire castle for the throne room, guessing that's where the king would be.

Ah, There he was, The great king of SparkPlug Island, Whose name is-

I don't know.

Maybe I'll call him Mah Lord.

Yeah.

You seriously need to show some respect.

So I went to the king and the first thing I did was (I hope you guessed it, because if you didn't, you're such a simp)

BOW.

I bowed down till my nose touched the ground, and then, I spoke.

"HELLO! MY LORD! I'm Robert, and uh, I just got teleported here by the tentacles dude...IT WASN'T MY FAULT-" But I got interrupted by some people coming from another door.

They looked teen-ish, and they looked like BFF's for life.

I just turned my head back to the king to ask 'Who are they again?' but that was a millisecond TOO late.

One kid from the group pointed a finger at me, and spoke in a dangerously calm voice.

"Who...are you?"

"Your MOM."

"Where did you come from?"

"Your head."

"SHUT UP. talk properly son."

"Fine. Name's Rob, and I come from LA."

I said.

"Okay...WHY DID YOU COME HERE?"

"Well, I got teleported...don't ask me why." I finished.

"WHY?"

"I SAID NOT TO ASK."

"JUST TELL."

"By the dude tentacles...look. I come from a normal day, until some people start chasing me and capture me, take me to some weird secret island, and out of nowhere tell me to save the world, which I DON'T AGREE TO. I'm a weakling. So yeah- then they put me to training, give me some powered enchanted sword, and order me to kill a bunch of giants. So after I killed them, I kind of got teleported here." I finished the last part annoyingly. I MEAN, HOW MANY TIMES YOU HAVE TO SAY THAT?

"Well...we'll try our best but-" Another guy started but was interrupted by a blood curdling scream.

I immediately took out howldanger, which glowed in the darkness and rushed to the courtyard.

Well, what was going on there wasn't a pretty scene. As soon as I came, an enormous banana came and almost crushed me, roaring in the process. My legs froze. For some reason they WOULDN'T move.

Finally I regained consciousness and stabbed the thing's leg. It vanished into thin air.

"OH MY GODS!! HELP!" came a scream, and i turned.

Well, oof. The king ran around helplessly chased by 50 bananas. Don't get me insanely wrong but, they look funny.

I screamed in battle cry.

"YAAAAAA! TASTE THE POWER OF HOWLDANGER!" I screamed, and every single banana turned to me, their mouths wide open and their expression totally MAD.

Every single part of my body screamed, RUN!!!

But I didn't. I raised HowlDanger into the sky, making waves bigger and thunder flash in the sky.

My eyes seemed to close.

Thunder boomed and hit the ground, making cracks and sonic booms.

The waves formed a tornado, and the wind pushed me forward, giving me a speed boost.

My body sparked with electricity, and I wondered what caused that.

Was it my sword? My imaginations? The gods? Was it-

The Lord of the Wild?

Oh boi.

For a moment I forgot everyone was staring at me, including the bananas.

But I guess it didn't work well.

All the bananas rushed at me, with swords in their hands.

Without hesitation, my body moved itself. Huh?

EXCUSE ME?

My legs rushed forward, and my head moved front.

WHAT?

WHAT'S HAPPENING?

My hand went up and my fingers tightened the grip on the hilt of howldanger.

I closed my eyes, feeling my body moving on its own, and when I finally opened them, all I saw was a bunch of dead bananas on the ground, their bodies sliced open in two.

"Ohh-KAY." I said quietly.

But I guess I must've screamed or something, because most of all the people staring at me were glaring.

"GUYS- I - ITS NOT WHAT IT SEEMS- I kind of- I mean, I NEVER TOOK TRAINING- Im not lying either, but uh- umm, what I mean is-" I babbled.

Out of nowhere, an arrow burst out and hit me on the chest. Well, then I blacked out.

I'm SORRY!

CHAPTER X

I hate this so, so much.

When I woke up, I couldn't feel myself. My eyes were opening up, getting used to the weather.

When my eyes finally opened up, what I saw wasn't a pretty scene.

I woke up on a beach, and I'm absolutely sure I'm not on SparkPlug island anymore. I put my hand on my chest, where the arrow had been lodged. It wasn't there. I wasn't surprised either.

I stood up, scanning the place.

OH, well. *cries*.

I'm back on to Terror of Death.

WHY?

WHY THIS OF ALL PLACES?

How did they know this place, I mean, the sparkplug people.

That question is way WAY too hard for someone like me, 'cause I gots only 108 iq.

Finally, after a million years of searching the beach, I found someone. Or atleast 10,000 people.

They gathered together?

What?

WHAT?

In front of the group, there lay another group.

The weird thing is, they all were armored and were holding swords-

Wait...NO.

THIS CAN'T BE HAPPENING!

One of them came to me, and he said, "Robert!! YEH BEEN GOOD?" HE'S KING!

"No, of course not. WHY DID YOU SEND ME TO SPARK PLUG ISLAND?" I yelled at his face, and he seemed surprised for a moment.

He backed a little, stumbling on a small rock, but regained his balance.

I glared right through his soul.

"What-" he started, but was interrupted by the battle cries of the armies, and they rushed forward, creating none other than World War III.

I took out my sword, put myself in position, and ran towards the armies of L'Terged.

AHAHA! CLIFFHANGER!
How I love cliffhangers.
The book is short but, there is a 2nd book,
Destiny 2: Arrival of the hunt.
I hope you liked the book! It's hard.
(Took me months to write! HELP!)
See you soon!
The End
A story by Abhinav, There's a part 2! Coming Soon.

Printed by Libri Plureos GmbH in Hamburg,
Germany